Lucky Break

MOLLY MAC

by MARTY KELLEY

This one is dedicated to The Fab Four: Laura, Jennifer, Pat and Beth. And to Bruce Johnson, who asked me to visit his school so many years ago – Marty

Published by Curious Fox, an imprint of Capstone Global Library Limited, 264 Banbury Road, Oxford, OX2 7DY - Registered company number: 6695582

www.curious-fox.com

Text © 2017 Marty Kelley
Illustrations © 2017 Marty Kelley

The author's moral rights are hereby asserted.

All characters in this publication are fictitious and any resemblance to real persons, living or dead, is purely coincidental.

ISBN 978 1 782 02702 7
21 20 19 18 17
10 9 8 7 6 5 4 3 2 1

A CIP catalogue for this book is available from the British Library.

Printed and bound in China.

Contents

Chapter 1
Luck! 7

Chapter 2
Luck Is Lost 12

Chapter 3
The Bad Day 19

Chapter 4
The Bad Day Gets Worse 26

Chapter 5
The Secret 34

Chapter 6
Sick Art 42

Chapter 7
Molly Mac, the Artist 48

Dad

Mum

Alex

Me

My Family by Molly Mac ARTIST!

All About Me!

A picture of me!

Name:

Molly Mac

People in my family:

Mum

Dad

Drooly baby brother Alex

My best friend: KAYLEY!!!!

I really like:

Crunchy delicious tacos!
But not if they have tomatoes on them.
Yuck! They are squirty and wet.

When I grow up I want to be:

An artist. And a famous animal trainer.
And a professional taco taster. And a teacher.
And a superhero. And a dinner lady. And a pirate!

My special memory: Kayley and I camped in my
garden. We toasted marshmallows with cheese.
They were surprisingly un-delicious.

Chapter 1

Luck!

Thunk. Thunk. Thunk, thunk, thunk.

"Molly Mac?" Kayley asked. "Do I even want to know what you're doing with Mr Rose's stamp?"

"Probably not," said Molly. She stamped her paper again. And again. And again.

Molly held up her paper to show Kayley. "I had to borrow Mr Rose's stamp that says 'Good Job!' I want everyone to know what a good job I did on my drawing."

Kayley looked at the picture. "What is it?" she asked.

Molly rolled her eyes. "It's a unicorn with a banana for a horn," she told her. "It's making a castle out of rainbow sprinkles. And **THAT** is the unicorn's puppy, Mr Sparkle Muffins."

Kayley nodded. "**Wow.** That's really good," she replied.

"Thanks!" Molly said. "I think it is all because of this."

Molly held up a pencil. "My Uncle Pat gave it to me last night," she said. "Look what it says on it!"

Kayley took the pencil and read it. "Lucky's Steakhouse."

Molly took the pencil back. "Lucky's!" she said. "Ever since he gave it to me, I've been having good luck. Last night, Uncle Pat took me out for ice cream. And this morning, I got extra jam on my toast. And I found 50p on the pavement. And we are having tacos for lunch today. And this is the best drawing I have ever done. I only rubbed one hole through the paper!"

"**Whoa,**" Kayley sighed. "**It IS lucky.**"

Mr Rose stood in front of the class. He held a piece of paper in his hand. "I have one announcement this morning," he said. "And it is very good news!"

Molly waved her pencil at Kayley. "My lucky pencil strikes again!" she said.

"Mr Putnam is having a school-wide art show," Mr Rose said.

"Does that mean we have to make art as wide as the school?" Molly asked.

"That's not what 'school-wide' means, Molly," replied Mr Rose.

"Is it going to be a TV show?" Molly asked. "Will we be TV stars?"

"No, Molly. It's an art show. Not a TV show," said Mr Rose. "Anyone can make art to enter in the show. The winner will get £10."

"£10? That's a fortune!" Molly cried. "If I win, I could finally buy an automatic taco maker! This is the best day ever!"

Chapter 2

Luck Is Lost

Briiiiiiing!

The bell rang for breaktime.

Molly grabbed her sketchbook and her lucky pencil. She stuffed them in her rucksack. Then she jumped up from her seat. "Come on, Kayley! Let's go!" she yelled.

Molly and Kayley raced out of the door. They bolted across the crowded playground. They zigged and zagged. They ran around the swings. They climbed up the slide and slid down. Finally, they zipped into their secret snack spot. That's where they ate a snack every day.

The two girls flopped down on the ground.
"Why were you running around like crazy?"
Kayley asked.

"I didn't want anyone to follow us," Molly
said. "I'm going to work on my art for the art
show. I don't want anybody to see it and copy it."

Kayley nodded. "Good idea," she said.

"My lucky pencil must be giving me good ideas, too!" Molly said. She unzipped her rucksack.

"What are you going to draw?" Kayley asked.

Molly took out her sketchbook. "I don't even know yet," she replied. "But I'm sure it will be incredible because of my new lucky pencil. I'll win the art show. And then I'll get £10 to buy that automatic taco maker!"

"Maybe you should draw a picture of a giant taco," Kayley said.

"**Yeah!**" Molly said. "A sparkly rainbow taco with hot fudge sauce and wings!"

Molly looked in her rucksack. She shoved
her hands into it and waved them around.

She tipped the rucksack upside down and
shook it.

"Do I even want to know what you're doing,
Molly?" asked Kayley.

Molly opened her empty rucksack to show
Kayley. **"My lucky pencil is gone!"** she yelled.

Molly and Kayley searched for Molly's lucky pencil. They zigged and zagged. They ran around the swings. They climbed up the slide and slid down.

They didn't find the lucky pencil.

"I'll ask some people to help us look," Kayley said.

Molly ran over to Ms Toth, the playground supervisor. "**I lost my lucky pencil!**" she told her. "It was in my rucksack. I was going to use it to win the art show. If I win the art show, I can finally buy an automatic taco maker. I even made sure nobody followed us to our secret spot, but the pencil is gone! Do you have a magnifying glass? I want to look for clues. Can you help me look for clues?"

Ms Toth took a big, slurpy sip of her coffee. "Good morning, Molly Mac," she said.

Molly shook her head. "It **was** a good morning," she said. "Now it's not good at all. **I lost my lucky pencil!** I will never win the art show without it."

"I will be happy to keep my eyes open for it, Molly," Ms Toth answered. "But you know you don't need a lucky pencil to win an art show, right?"

"I do need it!" Molly replied. "Ever since I got it, I have been **REALLY** lucky. I even found 50p this morning! See?" Molly shoved her hand in her pocket. Her finger poked through a hole.

"**It's gone!**" Molly cried. "My good luck is turning into bad luck without the pencil!"

Chapter 3

The Bad Day

Clink. Click. Clack.

Molly was back in class. She was busy
looking through boxes in the science corner.

"Molly Mac?" said Mr Rose.

"Don't ask," said Molly.

"I'm asking," Mr Rose answered. "Why are
you over here?"

"I lost the lucky pencil that my Uncle
Pat gave me," Molly said. "And I also lost the
money I found. That means that I lost my good
luck. I need to get my pencil back!"

"Do you think your missing pencil is over
here?" Mr Rose asked.

"Probably not," said Molly.

Mr Rose sighed. "So why are you over here, Molly?"

"I'm looking for a magnifying glass. I want to search for clues."

"Not now, Molly," Mr Rose said. "You need to go back to your seat. It's time for our spelling test."

"**Spelling test?**" Molly cried. "**Now? I didn't even study! How could my luck get any worse?**"

The loudspeaker beeped and crackled.

Mr Rose held his finger up to his lips. "The Magic Box speaks," he said.

"May I have your attention, please? Today's lunch menu has changed. We were going to have crunchy, delicious tacos today. Now we will be having vegetable soup instead. Thank you."

The loudspeaker beeped and popped off.

Molly slowly walked back to her seat.

Klunk.

She dropped her head onto her desk.

"Are you okay, Molly?" asked Kayley.

"This is the worst day ever!" Molly replied.

After the spelling test, the class went to the library. Mrs Ross read them a story. It was about a boy. He made friends with a lucky leprechaun.

When she finished reading, everyone got to pick out books.

Molly raced over to Mrs Ross. "Can I borrow that book, Mrs Ross?" she asked. "I seem to be out of luck. I think I need to catch a leprechaun to get my luck back."

Mrs Ross scratched her head. "Do I even want to know what you're talking about, Molly?" she asked.

"I lost my lucky pencil," said Molly. "And now I'm having bad luck. I need to learn how to catch a leprechaun. Then I can have good luck again. Maybe I'll find my money and win the art contest. I really want that automatic taco maker!"

Mrs Ross scratched her head again. "Nope. You lost me there, Molly," she said. "I still have no idea what you're talking about."

"I need to borrow that book. It will tell me how to catch a leprechaun," said Molly.

Mrs Ross shook her head. "This book is a made-up story, Molly," she told her. "It doesn't teach you how to catch leprechauns."

"Okay," Molly said. "Where are the books about how to catch leprechauns? I need some good luck."

Mrs Ross walked over to a shelf. She ran her finger along the books. Then she pulled one out. "Here you go. This book is about good luck charms."

Molly flipped through the pages. "I don't see anything in here about leprechaun traps," she said.

"No," said Mrs Ross. "You would need a leprechaun trapping licence for that, Molly."

"But I need some good luck," Molly said. "And I need it fast."

Mrs Ross flipped through the pages of the book. She pointed to the words at the top of one page, 'Good Luck Charms'. "Maybe this will help," she said.

Chapter 4

The Bad Day Gets Worse

Thud.

Kayley plonked her lunch tray on the table. She slid into her seat next to Molly. Molly waved her spork around slowly in front of her face. She looked at it very carefully. "Does this spork look lucky to you?"

"It looks like a spork," replied Kayley. "They all look the same."

"I think this one might be a lucky one," Molly said. She waved it around a bit. "Do you see any good luck sparkles dripping from it?"

"No," Kayley said. "Only vegetable soup." She wiped up the drops of soup.

"And vegetable soup is definitely not lucky," Molly sighed.

"No," Kayley agreed. "Especially not when we were supposed to have crunchy, delicious tacos."

Molly poked her spork into her soup and stirred. "My luck is getting worse and worse," she said.

"Really?" Kayley asked.

"Yep," said Molly. "Mrs Ross showed me a book with good luck charms in it. It didn't help at all. Did you know that some people think a rabbit's foot is good luck?"

"**Just the foot?**" Kayley gasped.

"Just the foot," replied Molly.

"**Yuck!**" said Kayley.

"I know!" Molly said. "I'm not going to steal a foot from a rabbit. What if he didn't wash between his toes? I need to find another lucky charm. Do you think this straw looks lucky?"

"No. Just milky," Kayley said.

"How about this napkin?" Molly waved her napkin in the air. Her arm knocked Mr Rose's lunch tray out of his hands as he walked by.

CRASH!

Mr Rose's shoes and trousers were covered in vegetable soup.

Molly gasped. She jumped up from her seat. "I'm so sorry, **Mr Roooh...ohhh...ooohh–**" Molly slipped in the soup. She tumbled backwards to the floor. "**My wrist!**" she cried as she landed on the soupy floor.

"That is definitely not a lucky napkin," Kayley said.

An hour later, Molly sat on the big white bench in the doctor's office. Paper crinkled and wrinkled beneath her. Molly's mother stood next to her. She had her arm around Molly's shoulders.

Dr Preble sat at a small desk. He looked at an X-ray of Molly's wrist.

"I have good news and bad news," Dr Preble said. "The good news is that your wrist isn't broken. The bad news is that you do have a very bad sprain. You will have to keep your arm in a splint and a sling until it gets better."

"Will it be better by tomorrow?" Molly asked. "I have some big plans. I really need my wrist for them."

Dr Preble smiled and shook his head. "I'm afraid not, Molly," he said. "I think your wrist will need a couple of weeks in the splint to get better."

Dr Preble gently wrapped Molly's wrist. He placed a sling over her shoulder.

"What about the art contest?" Molly asked. "How will I draw a picture with this thing on my wrist? Do you have a robotic arm I can use until mine is better? Maybe one that I can control with my mind? And one that will do my homework for me? And scratch my back?"

"I don't have anything like that, Molly," answered Dr Preble. "I do have some stickers, though. Would you like one?"

Molly nodded. "Yes, please."

Dr Preble opened a cupboard door. He took out a small red and white box. He held the box out in front of Molly. "**Oops. Sorry.** Looks like I've run out of stickers."

Chapter 5

The Secret

Schwwwwp...schwwwwp...schwwwwp...

"Molly? Do I even want to know why you're rubbing the light switch?" Uncle Pat asked. He had stopped by to visit when he had heard about her wrist.

"Probably not," replied Molly.

Molly walked to the other side of the living room. She rubbed another light switch.

"I think I definitely want to know," Uncle Pat said. He sat on the couch and waved Molly over. Molly walked over and sat down next to him. Uncle Pat put his arm around Molly's shoulder.

"I'm rubbing the light switches so a genie will appear," Molly said. "I need a genie to grant my wish."

"I think genies live in magic lamps, not light switches, Molly," said Uncle Pat.

Molly sighed. "I know, but we don't have any magic lamps," she said. "A light switch is the closest thing I could think of."

"I see," Uncle Pat said. "And what are you going to wish for if a genie appears?"

"I need some good luck," Molly said. "I lost your lucky pencil. Now I have really bad luck. First I lost my 50p. Then I didn't get a leprechaun book. I had to eat vegetable soup with a non-lucky spork. And I sprained my wrist and didn't even get a sticker! Now I can't enter the art contest or buy an automatic taco maker."

"**Wow,**" Uncle Pat said. "That's too bad."

"I know," Molly said. "I don't want to make you feel bad. But since you gave me the lucky pencil, this is kind of all your fault."

Uncle Pat smiled. "I see," he said. "Can I make it up to you by sharing a secret with you? Something that nobody else in the whole wide world knows?"

Molly thought for a minute. "Well, you can try," she replied. "I'm not sure if a secret will help. Ice cream might be a better way to make it up to me."

Uncle Pat shook his head. "No ice cream today, Molly," he said.

"See?" Molly said. **My luck just keeps getting worse and worse!**"

"**Shhhh,**" Uncle Pat whispered. "Let me tell you the secret."

Molly shuffled over on the couch.

"That wasn't a lucky pencil," Uncle Pat
whispered.

The next morning, Molly Mac waddled into
the kitchen. She had a pillow on her head. Two
more pillows were stuffed in her T-shirt.

Mum looked at her. "Molly?" she asked.

Just then, Alex squealed. "**Moowwww!**" Baby food sprayed out of his mouth. It hit Mum right in the face as she turned to look at him.

Mum wiped her face and looked at Molly.

"Don't ask," Molly said.

"I'm asking," Mum said.

"Uncle Pat told me the pencil he gave me wasn't even lucky," Molly said. "But he's wrong. Since I lost it, my luck has got worse and worse. I'm wearing these pillows to school today to keep me safe."

"No, you are not, young lady," Mum said. She pulled the pillows out of Molly's T-shirt. Then she lifted the pillow off Molly's head.

Molly slumped into a seat at the table. "I need those to protect me from bad luck," she said. "What if a piano falls out of the sky and squishes me?"

"I don't think a piano is going to fall from the sky while you're walking to school," Mum said. She handed Molly some yoghurt and a banana.

"What if a zoo train goes off the tracks? A load of animals could escape. **I could be eaten by a lion! Or a tiger! Or a monkey in a clown suit!** Anything could happen now that I lost my lucky pencil."

Mum sat next to Molly. She fed Alex some more of his baby food. "There are no train tracks anywhere near us, Molly. You do not need to worry about a monkey in a clown suit. And Uncle Pat was right. That wasn't a lucky pencil. Sometimes good things happen. Sometimes bad things happen. It isn't because of a lucky pencil. You have had a few bad things happen lately. But that doesn't mean you have bad luck."

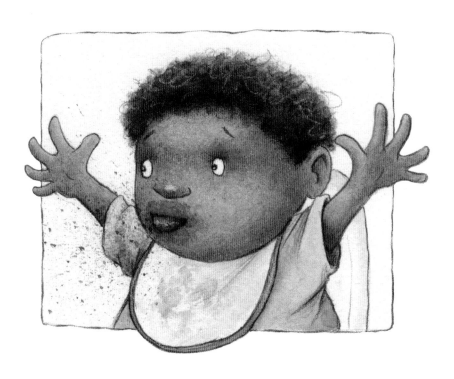

"**Pppffffttttttttttt!!!!!**" Alex sprayed a mouthful of baby food all over Molly and Mum.

"I definitely need those pillows today," Molly moaned.

Chapter 6

Sick Art

"**Wow!**" Kayley said when she saw Molly at school that day. "Is your arm broken?"

"Not yet," Molly said. "But my luck is getting worse and worse. I'm sure it will be broken by lunchtime. Unless a monkey in a clown suit eats me before then."

"Does it hurt?" asked Kayley.

"Only when I do this." Molly wiggled her fingers. "**Ouch!**"

Mr Rose walked over to Molly and Kayley. "Oh, my," he said. "Your mother called and told me about your wrist, Molly. I'm very sorry you hurt it. How are you feeling today?"

Molly sighed. "I'm okay," Molly replied.
"Unless I do this." She wiggled her fingers.
"Ouch!"

"Well, stop wiggling your fingers and line
up for art," Mr Rose said.

"Art?" Molly said. "I can't draw with this."
She wiggled her fingers again. **"Ouch!"**

The class walked down the corridor to the art room. Molly and Kayley took their seats.

"Good morning, class!" said the art teacher, Mr Putnam. "Today, I'm going to give you time to work on a project for the art show."

Molly raised her hand. "Mr Putnam! Mr Putnam!" she shouted. "I'm having a small emergency about the art show. I was planning on winning £10 to buy an automatic taco maker. But then I lost my lucky pencil. It was helping me do great drawings. Ever since then, I've been having really bad luck. A monkey in a clown suit may eat me before the art show even happens. And even if it doesn't, I can't win the art show. I can't draw a sparkly rainbow taco with hot fudge sauce and wings with this thing on my arm."

Molly wiggled her fingers. "**Ouch!**"

Mr Putnam walked over to Molly. "Molly, there are lots of ways to make art," he said.

"But my lucky pencil was making me a really good artist," Molly said. "The unicorn I drew looked just like a unicorn."

Mr Putnam walked over to his bookshelf. He brought a huge book over to Molly. He opened it and started to flip through the pages. "All artists work differently, Molly. Some artists want to create things that look real. Some artists try to share feelings in their art."

He showed Molly pictures of paintings. Some looked like splashes of colour. Others looked like a lot of shapes. And a few looked like squiggles and smears of paint.

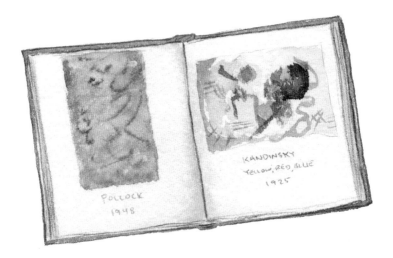

"Artists did those?" Molly asked. "They look like baby Alex's tray when he's finished eating!"

Mr Putnam smiled. "These are very famous pieces of art. Very famous artists made them. The artists were trying to show a feeling or an emotion. Not a thing."

"**Whoa...**," Molly gasped.

Mr Putnam pointed to Molly's left hand. "Maybe you could use your left hand to make a piece of art. It could show how you are feeling."

"Do you think a piece of art that looks like **baby sick** could win the art show?" Molly asked.

Mr Putnam shrugged. "Absolutely."

Molly Mac grabbed a paintbrush and got right to work.

Chapter 7

Molly Mac, the Artist

"**Come on! Come on! Come on!**" Molly Mac pulled Mum and Dad through the crowds at the school-wide art show. Alex gurgled and burped and smiled.

"We're coming, Molly! Don't pull my fingers off!" Dad laughed.

Molly led them down the hall. She stopped in front of her painting. "There it is!" she cried. She pointed to a big red ribbon next to her painting. "Second place! I won second place!"

"**Wow!**" Mum and Dad said. Dad scooped up Molly and gave her a big hug. "That's wonderful!"

Mum stepped up to the painting. She looked at it closely. "It shows a lot of feeling," she said.

"I tried to show how I was feeling about losing my lucky pencil," Molly told her. "Mr Putnam told us that we should name our paintings. I call this one **'I Lost My Lucky Pencil, But at Least I Didn't Get Eaten by a Monkey in a Clown Suit.'**"

Mum smiled. "You won second place," she said. "And you didn't even need that pencil from Uncle Pat."

"I know!" Molly cried. "I think this must be my lucky sling! I didn't win the £10 prize. But I'm going to use this lucky sling to help me get that automatic taco maker."

"Do I even want to know what you're planning, Molly Mac?" Dad asked.

"Probably not," she replied.

All About Me!

A picture of me!

Name:
Marty Kelley

People in my family:
My lovely wife, Kerri
My amazing son, Alex
My terrific daughter, Tori

I really like: Pizza! And hiking in the woods. And being with my friends. And reading. And making music. And travelling with my family.

When I grow up I want to be:
A rock star drummer!

My special memory:
Sitting on the sofa with my kids and reading a huge pile of books together.

Find more at my website: www.martykelley.com

MOLLY MAC

>Tooth Fairy Trouble<
by MARTY KELLEY

MOLLY MAC

>The Best Friend Bandit<
by MARTY KELLEY

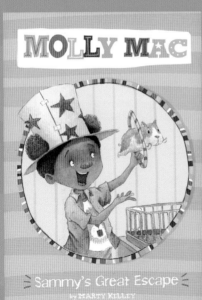

MOLLY MAC

>Sammy's Great Escape<
by MARTY KELLEY

For more exciting books from
brilliant authors, follow the fox!
www.curious-fox.com